SISKIYOU COUNTY LIBRARY
3 2871 00331027 9
DISCARDED

D0577046

Numblers

1
2 3
4 5 6
7 8 9 10

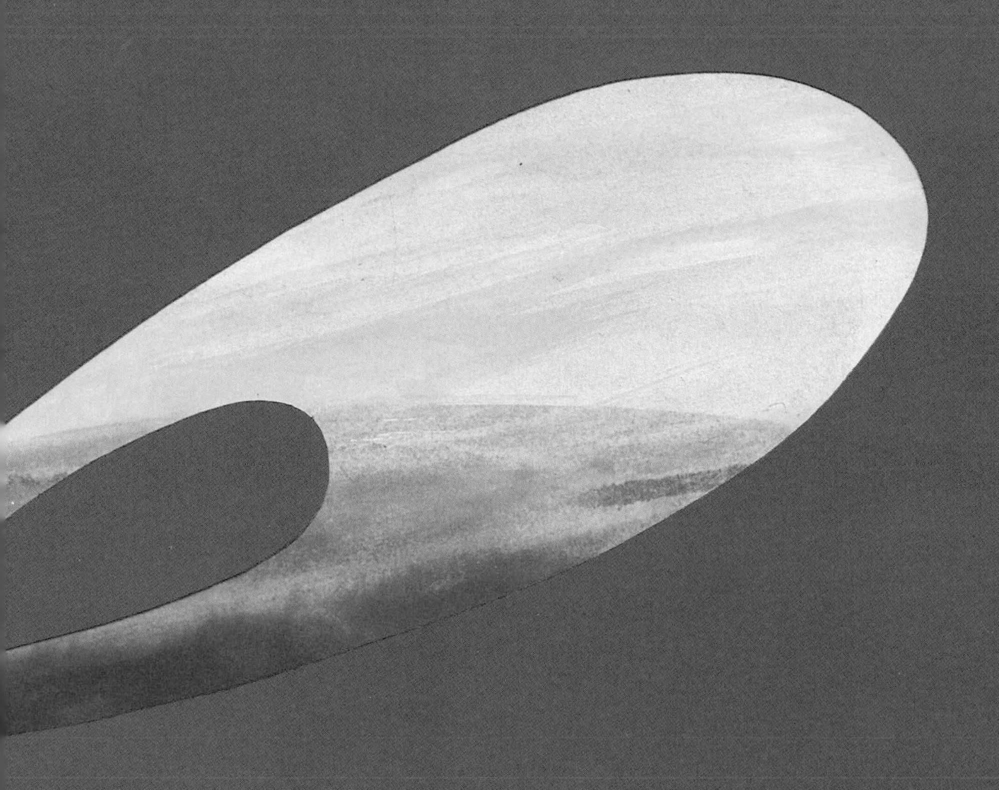

Numblers

Suse MacDonald
Bill Oakes

Dial Books for Young Readers * New York

To seeing in many dimensions.
—S.M. and B.O.

Published by Dial Books for Young Readers
A Division of NAL Penguin Inc.
2 Park Avenue, New York, New York 10016

Published simultaneously in Canada
by Fitzhenry & Whiteside Limited, Toronto

Designed by the authors
Typography by the authors and Amelia Lau Carling
Printed in the U.S.A.
(a)
First Edition
10 9 8 7 6 5 4 3 2 1

Library of Congress Cataloging in Publication Data
MacDonald, Suse. Numblers.
Summary: On each double-page spread a number from one to ten changes gradually into a familiar object or animal, splitting apart in the process into the appropriate number of parts or pieces. Descriptive text in the back gives clues as to the nature of the thing depicted.
1. Counting—Juvenile literature. [1. Counting.]
I. Oakes, Bill. II. Title.
QA113.M33 1988 513′.2 [E] 87-32736
ISBN 0-8037-0547-6
ISBN 0-8037-0548-4 (lib. bdg.)

The full-color artwork was created in three layers from plain colored paper over hand-textured sheets with an acetate overlay. It was then color-separated and reproduced as red, blue, yellow, and black halftones.

Numbers have a definite shape and a definite size when you look at them, but in the blink of an eye they can do the unexpected. That's when they become Numblers. With a shimmer and a stretch, each number becomes part of a picture, displaying qualities you'd think it would have and ones you'd never imagine. You'd expect a picture made up of *fives* to have five parts…but would you expect it to become a train? You'd expect a "three" picture to have three parts, but would you expect a frog? Each of these transformations gives the readers a surprise, plus the challenge of counting up the parts. It takes a spirit of adventure and a big imagination to keep up with these Numblers, but if you need any help, there's a key at the back!

one

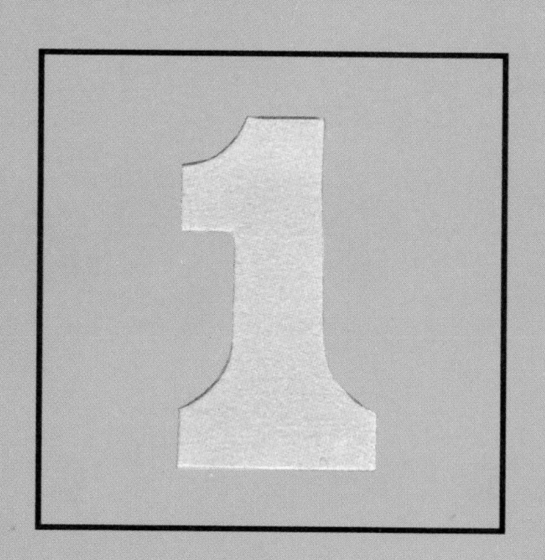

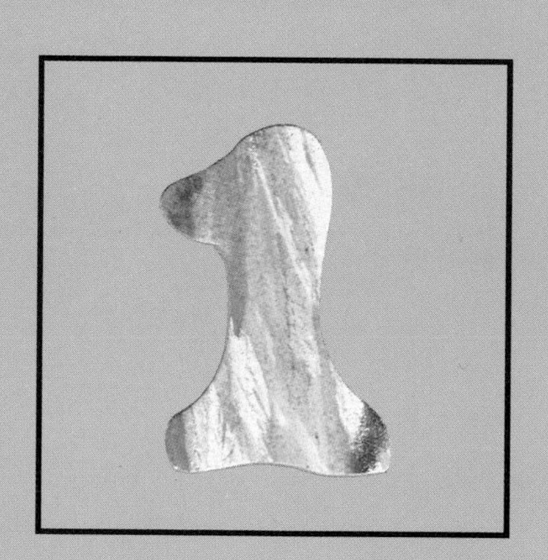

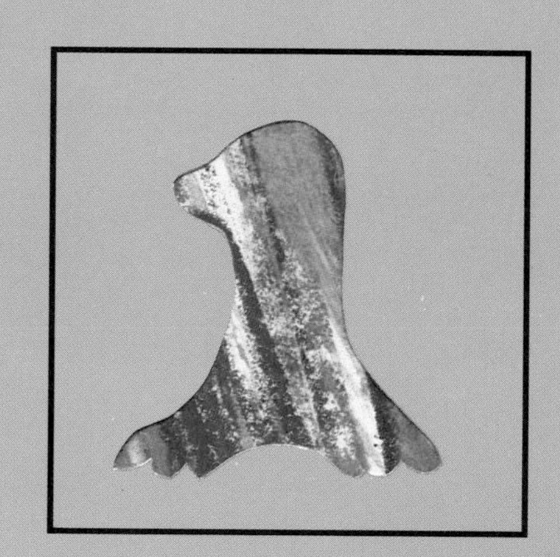

two

2

three

3

four

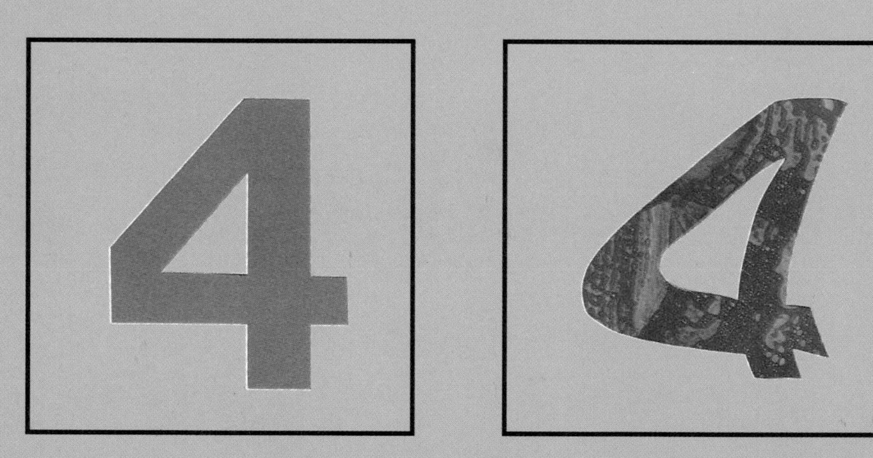

five

six

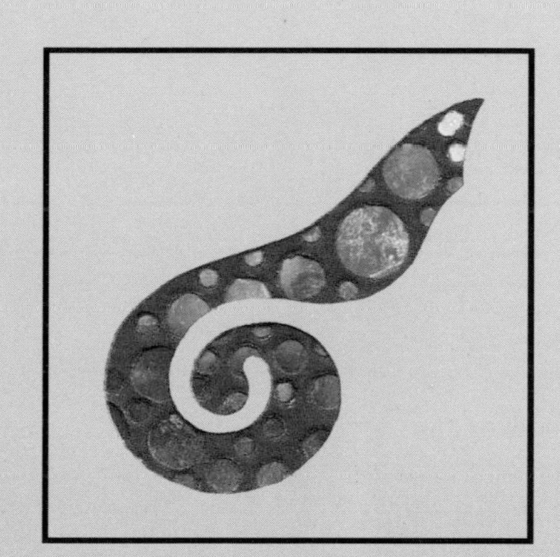

seven

eight

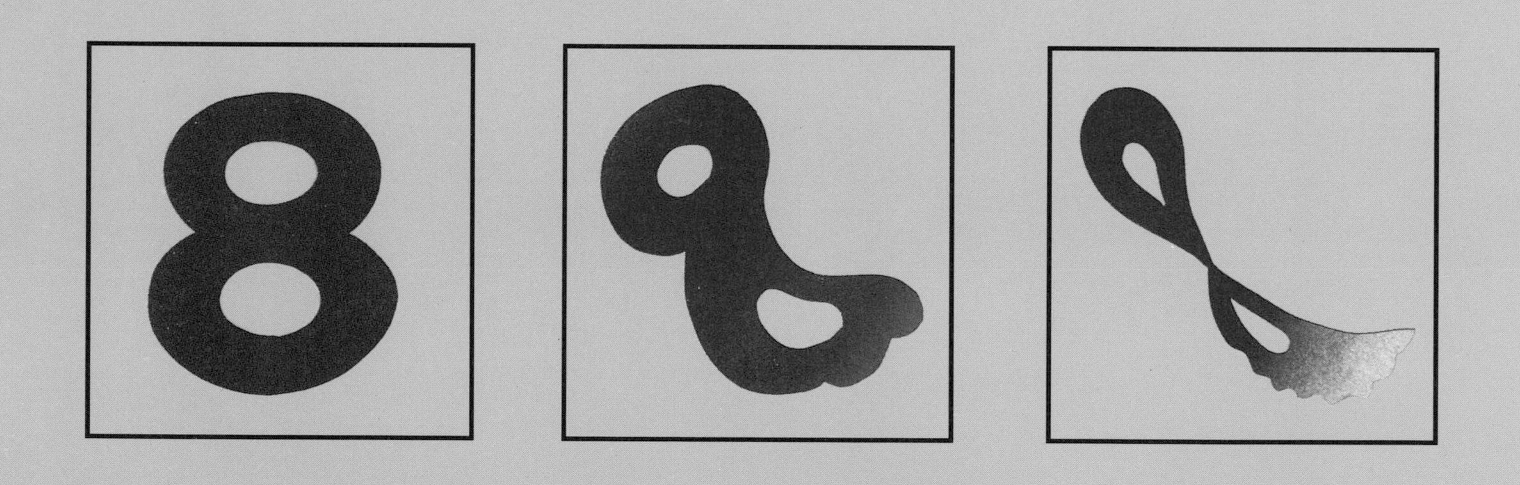

nine

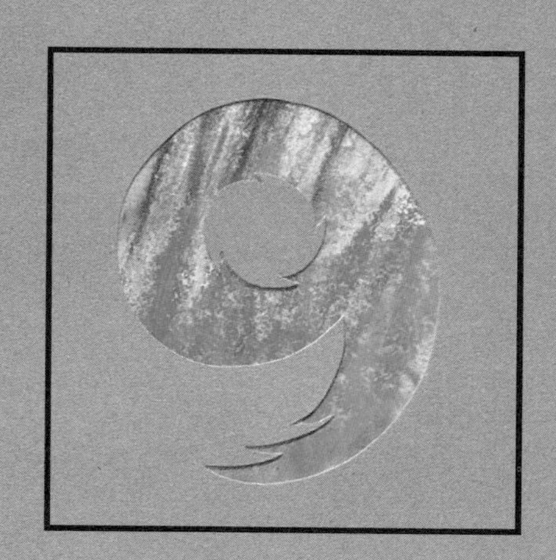

ten

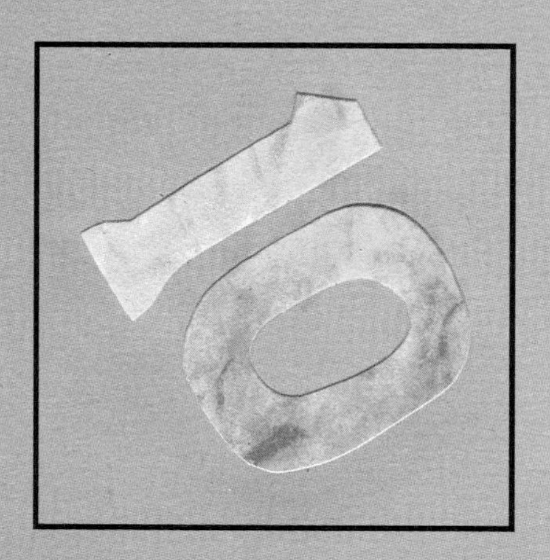

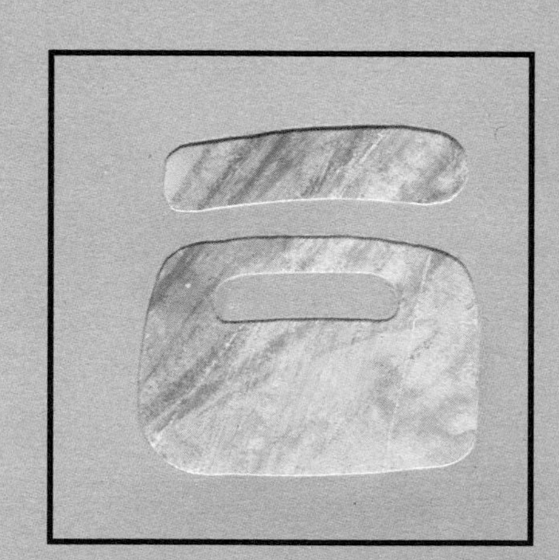

Where to Find the Numbers

The airplane to the left uses *eights* as its parts. If you count them, you find an *eight* as the tail, the body, the wings, the pilot's face, the engine, the propeller, and both of the airplane's wheels; eight *eights* in all!
A key to the rest of the pictures is below:

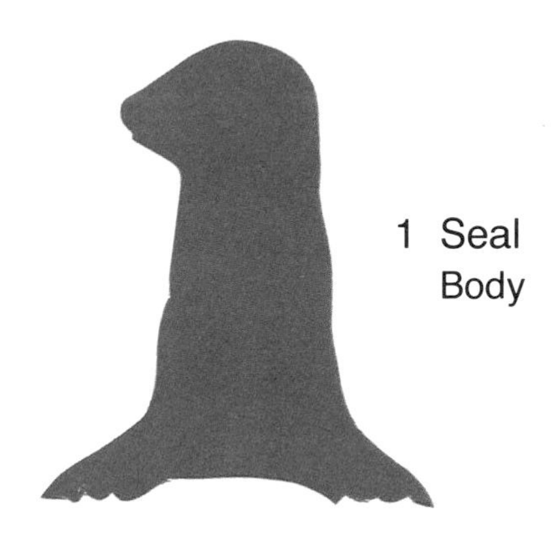

1 Seal
Body

3 Frog
Head, leg, leg

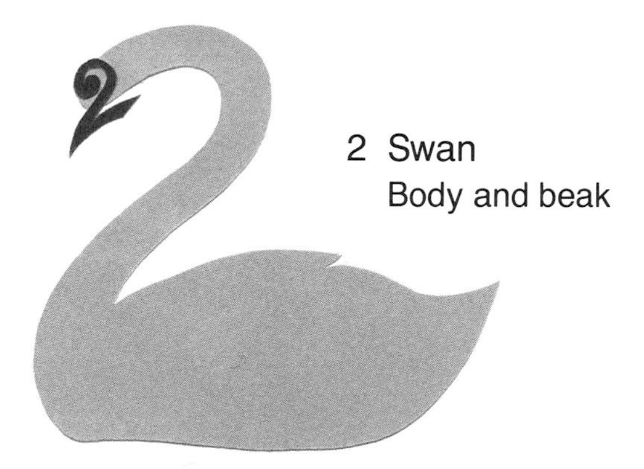

2 Swan
Body and beak

4 Sailboat
Flag, sail, sail, hull

5 Locomotive
Back, middle, engineer (under the top of the middle *five*), front, smokestack

8 Butterfly
Antenna, antenna, head and wing, leg, leg, body and wing, wing marking, wing marking

6 Sea Horse
Ear, eye, nose, chin, back, stomach

9 Squirrel
Ear, ear, head, arm, nose, eye, foot, body, tail

7 Indian Chief
Nose, eye, chin, headband, feather, feather, feather

10 Hot Air Balloon
Basket, sandbag weights, body-head, arm-head, balloon, balloon decorations repeated five times

Suse MacDonald

grew up in Glencoe, Illinois, and earned a B.A. from the State University of Iowa. Her early art training included textbook illustration and ten years of work as a draftsman and designer, before her love of illustration prompted a return to art studies in Boston and her first book, *Alphabatics.* She now works with three other artists in a studio called "Round the Bend," and lives with her husband and two children in Vermont.

Bill Oakes

is the author of five books of visual exercises for art teachers and students. He studied art at the Cornish School of Applied Art and the Burnley School of Art, and holds a master's degree from the University of Massachusetts at Boston in critical and creative thinking—areas he would like to explore with his innovative approach to picture books. He is the father of two children and lives in New Hampshire.